The Night Before Christmas

The Night Before Christmas

WRITTEN BY Clement C. Moore

PAINTINGS BY Eric Puybaret

MACMILLAN
CHILDREN'S BOOKS

'Twas the night before Christmas,

when all through the house
not a creature was stirring,
not even a mouse;

The stockings were hung
by the chimney with care,
in hopes that St. Nicholas
soon would be there;

The children were nestled
all snug in their beds,

While visions of sugarplums
danced in their heads;

And Mama in her kerchief,
and I in my cap,
had just settled our brains
for a long winter's nap—

When out on the lawn
there arose such a clatter,
I sprang from my bed
to see what was the matter.

Away to the window
I flew like a flash,
tore open the shutters
and threw up the sash.

The moon on the breast
of the new-fallen snow,
gave the luster of mid-day
to objects below;

When, what to my wondering
eyes should appear,
but a miniature sleigh,
and eight tiny reindeer,

With a little old driver,
so lively and quick,
I knew in a moment
it must be St. Nick.

More rapid than eagles
his coursers they came,
and he whistled, and shouted,
and called them by name;

"Now *Dasher,*
now *Dancer,*
now *Prancer,*
and *Vixen*!

On *Comet,*
on *Cupid,*
on *Donner,*
and *Blitzen*!

To the top of the porch,
to the top of the wall!
Now, dash away,
dash away,
dash away all!"

As dry leaves that before
the wild hurricane fly,
when they meet with an obstacle,
mount to the sky.

So, up to the house-top
the coursers they flew,
with a sleigh full of toys—
and St. Nicholas too.

And then in a twinkling
I heard on the roof,
the prancing and pawing
of each little hoof.

As I drew in my head,
and was turning around,
down the chimney St. Nicholas
came with a bound.

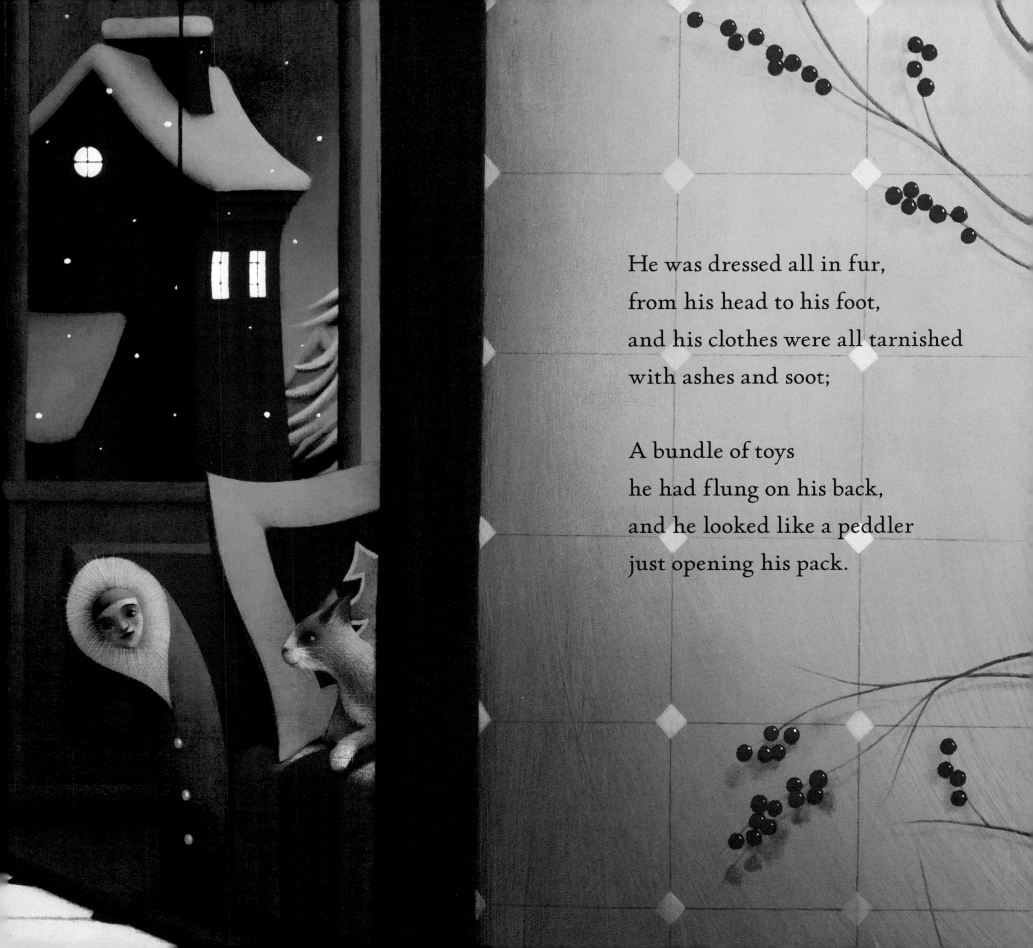

He was dressed all in fur,
from his head to his foot,
and his clothes were all tarnished
with ashes and soot;

A bundle of toys
he had flung on his back,
and he looked like a peddler
just opening his pack.

His eyes—how they twinkled!
His dimples how merry!
His cheeks were like roses,
his nose like a cherry!

His droll little mouth
was drawn up like a bow,
and the beard on his chin
was as white as the snow;

The stump of a pipe
he held tight in his teeth,
and the smoke, it encircled
his head like a wreath.

He had a broad face,
and a little round belly
that shook when he laughed,
like a bowl full of jelly.

He was chubby and plump—
a right jolly old elf,
and I laughed when I saw him,
in spite of myself;

A wink of his eye,
and a twist of his head,
soon gave me to know
I had nothing to dread.

He spoke not a word,
but went straight to his work,
and filled all the stockings;
then turned with a jerk,

And laying his finger
aside of his nose,

And giving a nod,
up the chimney he rose.

He sprang to his sleigh,
to his team gave a whistle,
and away they all flew,
like the down of a thistle;

But I heard him exclaim,
ere he drove out of sight,

"Merry Christmas
to all, and to all
a good night!"

For Mary—In thanks for the gift of you in our lives. —Peter and Noel Paul

For Camille — Eric

Performers' Note

On the wintry Rhode Island night in the 1820s when Clement C. Moore wrote the poem "'Twas the Night Before Christmas," he could not have foreseen that nearly two hundred years later, just a short stroll from Moore's original house, co-composers Noel Paul Stookey and Matthew Quinn would create a melody for his poem. In 1983, Noel brought the piece to Peter and Mary just in time for the first annual Holiday Concert at Carnegie Hall. Years later, Mary was intrigued when approached by Peter to record a spoken version of the original poem. Peter recalls, "I arrived at Mary's home with Kevin Salem, our engineer-producer for the 'Twas the Night Before Christmas' project who brought a simple rig to record Mary's voice in her Connecticut home. Though her health was very fragile, Mary's spirit was bright, just as it was during our last concerts when we shared some of our closest moments. Kevin's gentleness toward Mary put her at ease and made up for the improvised recording studio that neither she, nor we, were used to. With a habitual toss of her hair and a smile of delight, though without her long golden locks that had become so famous, she began reading to an imaginary child seated before her. She whispered, as if telling the child a secret or intimating that it was almost bedtime. When she finished, we were breathless, but in the manner of all recording sessions, she suggested we do another take. When we listened to both versions, it was obvious the first one had the heart, though the second was more polished. Mary turned to us and laughed, "You know, it's One-take Mary." And so the recording session ended, followed by a promise to Mary that we would create a very special musical background track for her reading. And we kept our promise."

Artist's Note

The figure of Santa is like a symbol of childhood reverie. So I had to respect it, to make it look like the classical imagery, but at the same time make it my own. How could I give my own child's fantasy to this very familiar character? That was the question. And then I wanted to find a context and abounding décor for this eternal story. I hope you enjoy the world I've created.

First published in the USA 2010 by Imagine Publishing Inc.
First published in the UK 2010 by Macmillan Children's Books
This edition published 2015 by Macmillan Children's Books
an imprint of Pan Macmillan
20 New Wharf Road, London N1 9RR
Associated companies throughout the world
www.panmacmillan.com

ISBN: 978-1-5098-0227-2

Written by Clement C. Moore
Illustrations copyright © Eric Puybaret 2010

CD copyrights and details

"Twas the Night Before Christmas"
Vocal and guitar by Noel Paul Stookey
New music by Noel Paul Stookey & Matthew Quinn © 1988 Neworld Media Music Publishers
Use courtesy of Rhino Entertainment Company (a Warner Music Group Company)

"Christmas Eve with Mary" (narrative version of "The Night Before Christmas")
Vocal narration by Mary Travers
Vocals and guitar by Peter Yarrow & Noel Paul Stookey
Orchestral arrangement by Kevin Salem
Produced, mixed and mastered by Kevin Salem, Woodstock, NY
Music by Noel Paul Stookey, Matthew Quinn, Peter Yarrow, Kevin Salem © 2010 Neworld Media Music Publishers (ASCAP),
© 2010 Mary Beth Music (ASCAP), © 2010 Van Rier Music (BMI)

"A' Soalin"
Vocals and guitar by Peter, Paul and Mary
Bass by Dick Kniss
Music by Stookey/Batteaste/Mezzetti
© 1963 Neworld Media Music Publishers (ASCAP)

Moral rights asserted.

3 5 7 9 8 6 4 2

A CIP catalogue record for this book is available from the British Library.

Printed in China

The illustrations in this book were printed using acrylic on linen.
Edited by Brooke Dworkin

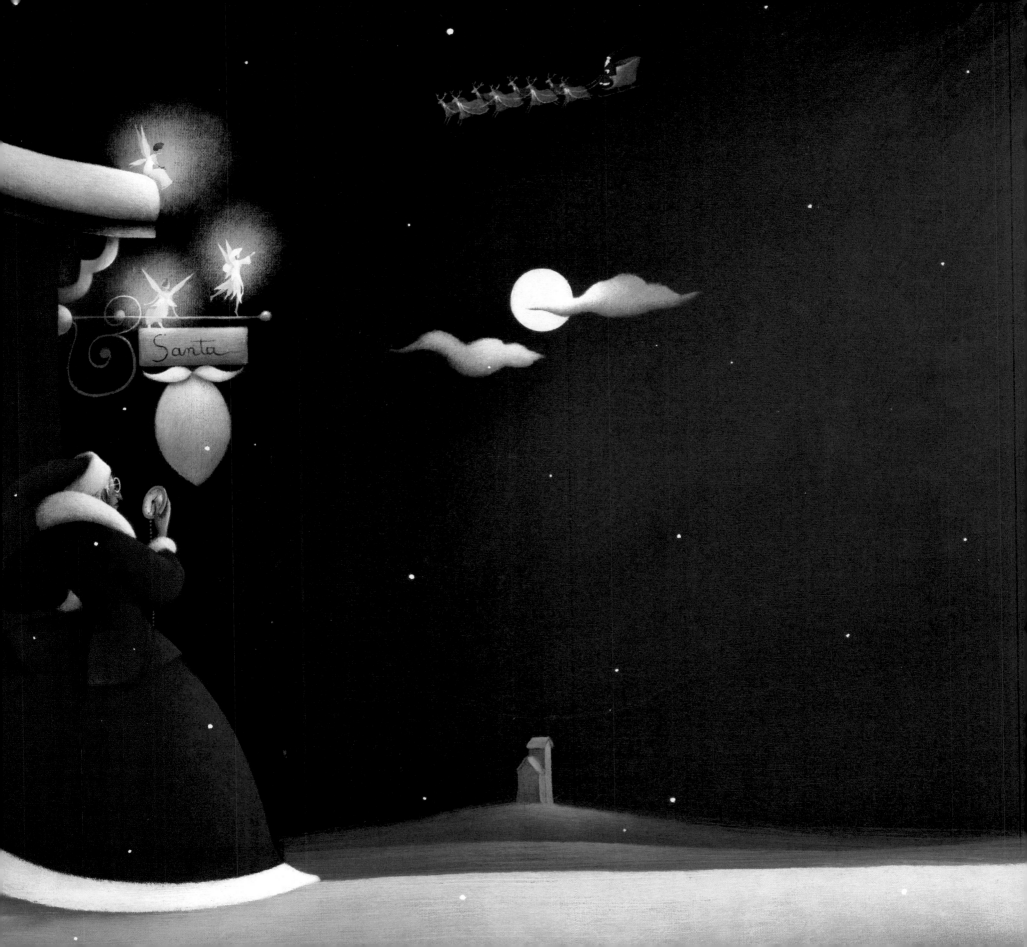